Underpants, thunderpants!

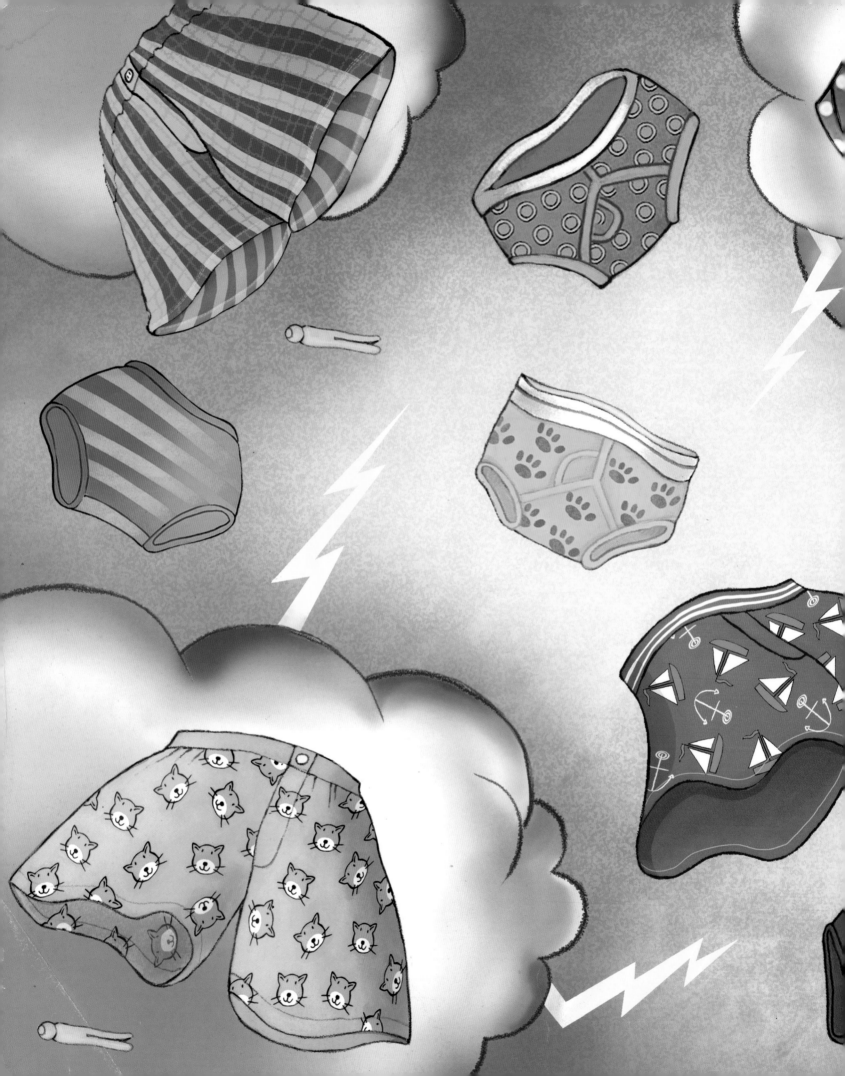

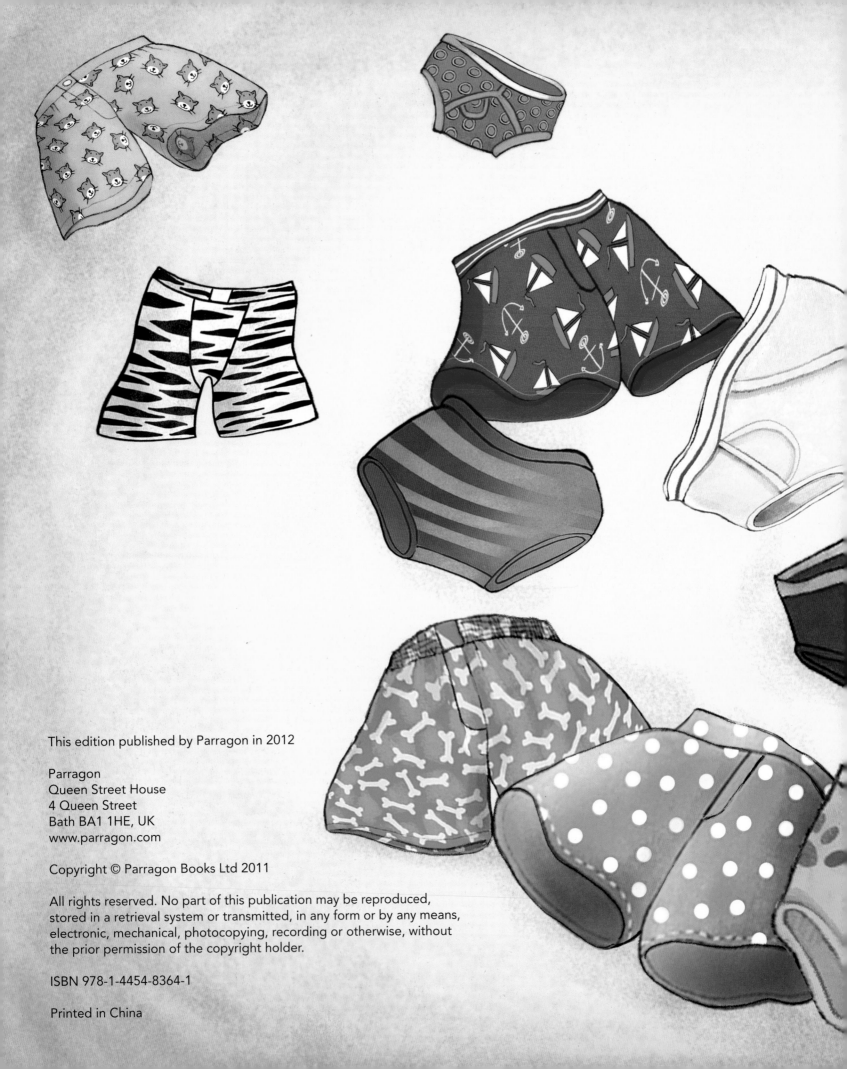

This edition published by Parragon in 2012

Parragon
Queen Street House
4 Queen Street
Bath BA1 1HE, UK
www.parragon.com

ISBN 978-1-4454-8364-1

Printed in China

Underpants, thunderpants!

Words by
peter Bently

Pictures by Deborah Melmon

PaRRagon

Bath · New York · Singapore · Hong Kong · Cologne · Delhi
Melbourne · Amsterdam · Johannesburg · Auckland · Shenzhen

One day
when the weather is
sunny and **fine**,
DOG hangs his
underpants
out on the line.

But **thunder** and **lightning**
soon fill up the sky.
underpants,
thunderpants!
Look at them
fly!

Over the **OCEAN**, the **JUNGLE** and **TOWN** — where will those **UNDIES** come **fluttering** down?

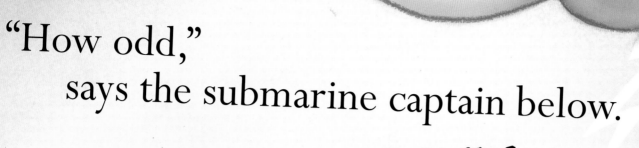

"How odd,"
    says the submarine captain below.

        "First I saw **lightning**

            and now I see **snow!**"

hello!

Down in the **sea,**
not far from the beach,
"A giant!
A giant!"
the little fish
screech.

Octopus **wriggles** and **jiggles** with **glee**.

"**Four** pairs of **underpants** perfect for me!"

underpants, plunderpants!

Just imagine that!

Roger the Pirate
has got a
new **hat!**

Safe out of sight of the **croc's** hungry eyes, Monkey's discovered a **cunning** disguise!

Elephant's **trunk** has been **tickled** by bees. **"Oh bother,"** he grumbles. "I'm going to **sneeze,** but I don't have a tissue. **What** shall I do?"

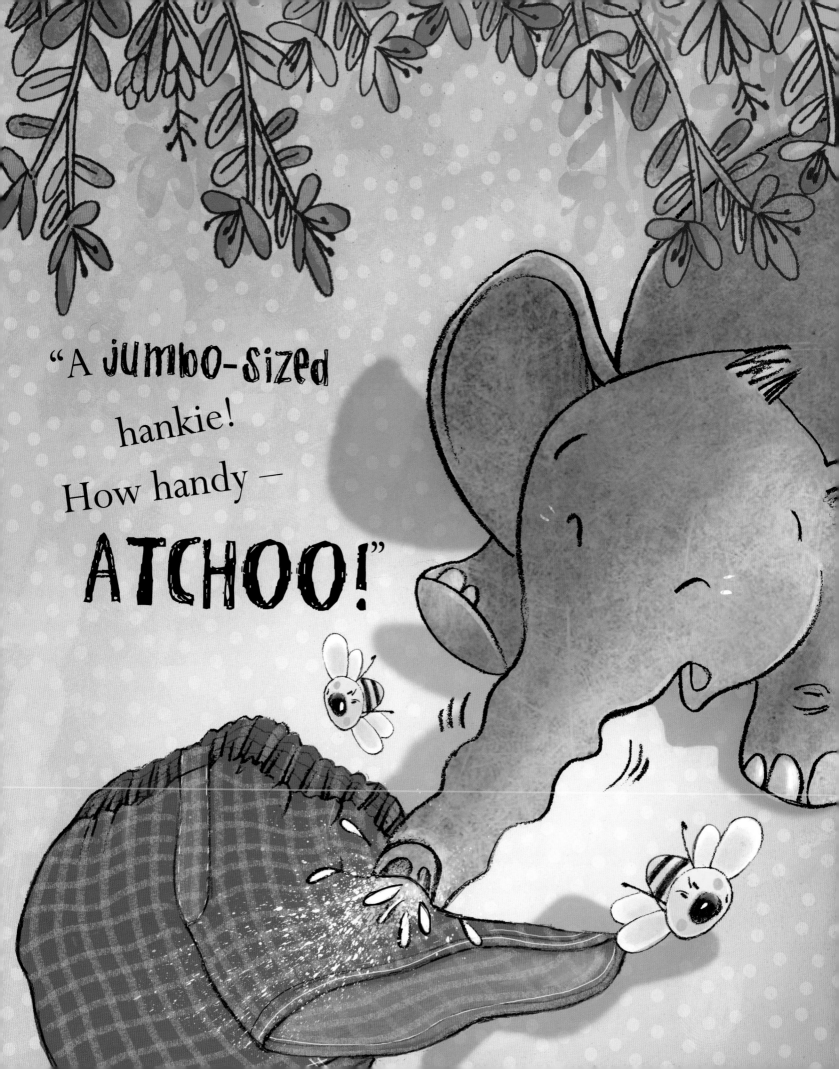

"A **jumbo-sized** hankie! How handy –

ATCHOO!"

Up at the **palace**, the **King** says, "**Oh my!** **Three** pairs of **underpants** baked in a pie!"

A **two-headed** alien stares from his **lair**...

"Underpants, wonderpants! Now I'm not **bare!**"

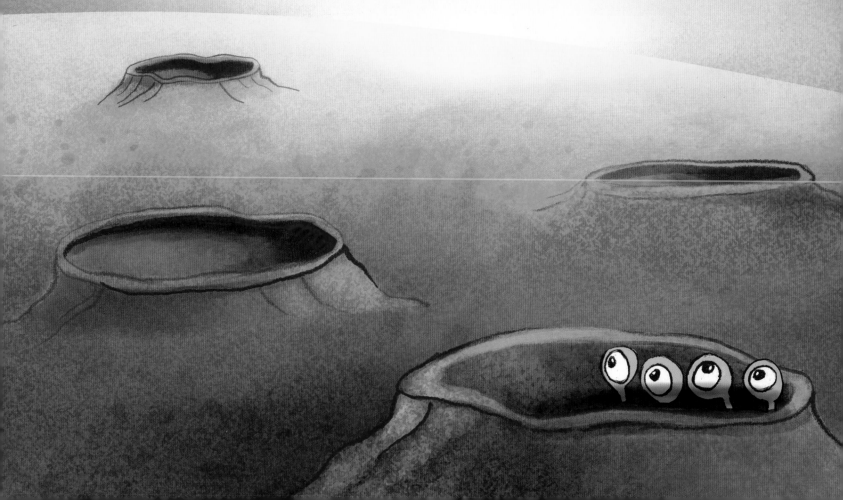

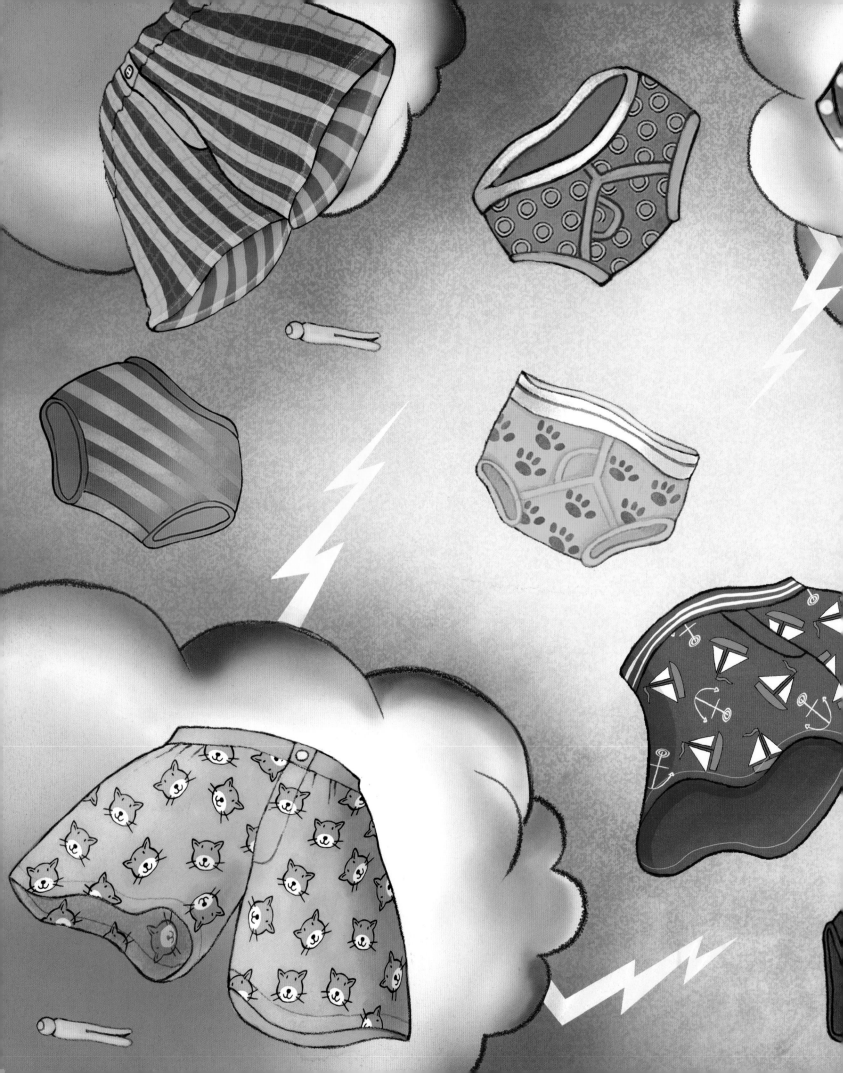

The
end